"Hey buddy, what's your number?" said a metal voice with a Brooklyn accent.

"I think that vacuum cleaner is talking to you," said Fred.

It was floating in midair right in front of us. And Fred was right. It did look kind of like an overgrown vacuum cleaner. The robot-vacuum thing floated closer. A beam of light shot out of its head and swept over us from head to toe. It raised one arm and pointed something at us that looked an awful lot like a laser gun.

"Don't shoot. We surrender. Take us to your leader," said Sam, holding up both hands.

"Hey buddy, what's your number?" Another robot arm extended a number pad at us.

"Give it a number," said Sam. "Quick!"

I punched in my phone number.

The red light blinked three times. "Wrong number."

Fred kicked the back of the robot. "Maybe we can knock out its power."

The red light blinked again. "You got five seconds, buddy."

Sam covered his head with both arms. "I can't believe I'm going to be zapped by a vacuum cleaner. Good-bye, cruel world."

"Three, two, one," said the robot. It jetted back a bit to get us all in its sights, then pointed its weapon directly at us.

THE TIME WARP TRIO

2095

by Jon Scieszka

illustrated by Lane Smith

PUFFIN BOOKS

In memory of Dean Alexander E. Nagy—
teacher, historian, scholar, giant

PUFFIN BOOKS
Published by the Penguin Group
Penguin Books USA Inc., 375 Hudson Street, New York, New York 10014, U.S.A.
Penguin Books Ltd, 27 Wrights Lane, London W8 5TZ, England
Penguin Books Australia Ltd, Ringwood, Victoria, Australia
Penguin Books Canada Ltd, 10 Alcorn Avenue, Toronto, Ontario, Canada M4V 3B2
Penguin Books (N.Z.) Ltd, 182-190 Wairau Road, Auckland 10, New Zealand

Penguin Books Ltd, Registered Offices: Harmondsworth, Middlesex, England

First published in the United States of America by Viking,
a division of Penguin Books USA Inc., 1995
Published in Puffin Books, 1997

14 15 16 17 18 19 20

THE LIBRARY OF CONGRESS HAS CATALOGED THE VIKING EDITION AS FOLLOWS:
Scieszka, Jon.
2095 / by Jon Scieszka ; illustrated by Lane Smith.
p. cm.—(The time warp trio)
Summary: While on a field trip to New York's Museum of Natural History,
Joe, Sam, and Fred travel one hundred years into the future, where they
encounter robots, anti-gravity disks, and their own grandchildren.
ISBN 0-670-85795-5
[1. Time travel—Fiction. 2. Museums—Fiction. 3. Field trips— Fiction.
4. New York (N.Y.)—Fiction.] I. Smith, Lane, ill. II. Title.
III. Series: Scieszka, Jon. Time warp trio.
PZ7.S41267Aaf 1995 [Fic]—dc20 94–44068 CIP AC

Puffin Books ISBN 0-14-037191-5

Printed in the United States of America

Other books in
THE TIME WARP TRIO series

ONE

"**H**ey buddy, what's your number?" said a metal voice with a Brooklyn accent.

"I think that vacuum cleaner is talking to you," said Fred.

I looked around the small room. There was an old-fashioned phone on the desk, big round glass lamps, and one of those record players with a hand crank that you see in history books. It looked like a room from a hundred years ago.

The only piece that seemed out of place was the metal thing floating in midair right in front of us. And Fred was right. It did look kind of like an overgrown vacuum cleaner.

The robot-vacuum thing floated closer. A beam of light shot out of its head and swept over us from head to toe.

"Hey buddy, what's your number?"

"It *was* the vacuum talking," said Fred.

"I don't think that's a vacuum," Sam whispered. "I'll bet it's a police robot. And now it's going to blast us with its death laser if we don't give it our numbers."

"I don't understand," I said. "We tapped the magic square to go one hundred years into the future. But except for the robot, it looks like we've gone one hundred years into the past."

Sam rolled his eyes. "What a surprise. We've never had any trouble with *The Book* before."

The droid floated closer. Its metal voice sounded meaner now.

"Hey buddy, what's your number?"

"Let's run for it," said Sam.

We moved left. The robot moved left.

We moved right. The robot moved right.

"Joe, you're the magician," said Fred. "Talk to it. Show it a trick. Give it some dust balls to suck up."

I didn't know exactly what to say to a robot, but I figured a trick might impress it.

"Hello Mr. Vacuum—or Robot—Guy. Have you ever seen a human bend metal?" I took a quarter out of my pocket and tapped it on the table. "Solid, right?" I held it out in front of me, at opposite edges, between the tips of my thumbs and forefingers. "Observe."

A little red light on the robot's head blinked.

I wiggled the quarter back and forth until it looked like it was bending. "Now I'll straighten it out." I stopped and pretended to press the quarter flat. "Pretty amazing, huh?"

The red light on the robot's head blinked twice. It raised one arm and pointed something at us that looked an awful lot like a laser gun.

"Don't shoot. We surrender. Take us to your leader," said Sam, holding up both hands.

"Hey buddy, what's your number?" Another robot arm extended a number pad at us.

"Give it a number," said Sam. "Quick!"

I punched in my phone number.

The red light blinked three times. "Wrong number."

Fred kicked the back of the robot. "Maybe we can knock out its power."

The red light blinked three times. "You got five seconds, buddy."

Sam covered his head with both arms. "I can't believe I'm going to be zapped by a vacuum cleaner. Good-bye, cruel world."

"Three, two, one," said the robot. It jetted back a bit to get us all in its sights, then pointed its weapon directly at us.

TWO

But before the Time Warp Trio meets its end by vacuum cleaner, let me freeze time, then go back in time to explain how we got to this time.

It was all our teacher's fault. It was Mr. Chester's brainstorm to take our class on a field trip to the American Museum of Natural History "To learn about how to live in the future from how people used to live in the past." That's what he said. Honest. We had to write it down on our Museum Worksheet.

Now don't get me wrong. I love the Museum. It's one of the best places in New York City. They've got a prehistoric alligator skull that's bigger than you, a herd of charging stuffed elephants, and a car with a hole in it from where it got bashed by a meteorite. If you sit close enough to the animal exhibits, it feels like you're right in the jungle or the mountain or the desert. And on hot summer days I like to go sit under the blue whale hanging from the ceiling in the ocean life room. It's blue, and quiet, and cool. And it has an excellent pack of killer whales.

But going to the museum on a class trip is a whole different story. You can't go look at the war clubs in the Iroquois longhouse. You can't hang around the stuffed gorillas. And you can never check out the rubber ants in the gift shop. You always have to stay together and answer the questions on the dreaded Museum Worksheet.

So there we were—standing under the huge Barosaurus skeleton in the museum lobby with our whole class, listening to Mr. Chester.

". . . which some people didn't even believe existed. Does anyone know its name? It says *Barosaurus* on the plaque. Right. Now we'll go in and look at the exhibits that show how people lived from 1890 up to 1990. Take a look and think about what things have changed in a hundred years. Stay together. You can either take notes for your worksheet or write out the complete answers as we go. Questions? No, you cannot check out the rubber ants in the gift shop."

The whole mob of us trailed behind Mr. Chester. We stopped at the 1890s room. There was an old-fashioned phone on the desk, big round glass lamps, and one of those record players with a hand crank that you see in history books. A lady mannequin dressed in a long dress stood by the table. A boy and a girl model were posed on the floor surrounded by marbles, checkers, and jacks.

"Oh boy," whispered Fred. "Just what I was hoping to see. Dummies dressed in old clothes."

"How did those poor kids live?" said Sam. "No TV, no Walkman, no computer, no fun."

"But look," said Fred. "That ad out the window

says BEER 5¢. I'll bet pizza was a penny."

". . . and changed the way people lived," Mr. Chester droned on. "Question Two on your sheet says, 'List five inventions we use today that people didn't use one hundred years ago.' Can anyone tell me one?"

Sam's hand shot up.

"Yes, Sam?"

"The zipper, invented by W. L. Judson in 1893. Or the electric vacuum cleaner, invented by Hubert Cecil Booth in 1901. Or the airplane the Wright brothers flew for the first time in 1903. Or frozen peas—"

"Thank you, Sam—"

"—invented by Clarence Birdseye in 1924. Scotch Tape, invented in 1929. And—"

"*Thank you*, Sam," said Mr. Chester.

Mr. Chester led our class to the next room. Fred, Sam, and I slowly worked our way to the back of the class, then sat down on a ledge in the 1920s room. Three gangsters were loading boxes. One held his machine gun ready.

"You've been reading the almanac again, haven't you?" asked Fred.

"How could you tell?" said Sam.

"Do you have a book of world records too?"

asked Fred. "I love that stuff like the biggest pizza ever."

"122 feet, 8 inches in diameter," I said, flipping a quarter up in the air.

"Wow," said Fred. "Now that's the kind of question I wouldn't mind answering."

I held up the quarter. "Would you like to see me bend metal with a little magic?"

Fred took out his Museum Worksheet. "No. But I would like to see you fill out this worksheet with a little magic. Why do we have to answer this stuff anyway? We should tell Mr. Chester if he really wants to find out this junk, he should travel back a hundred years with *The Book*."

"I'm sure that would go over big," said Sam. "Just like Joe's excuse that we couldn't do our math homework because we almost got run over by a woolly mammoth."

"Or your history paper on Blackbeard's awful singing," I said. "That was a real winner."

"What we really need," said Sam, "is someone who can show us how to use *The Book* the right way. Then we can travel around in time without worrying about getting killed while we look for *The Book* to get us home."

"Yeah," said Fred. "Whatever happened to your

uncle Joe? He gave you *The Book*. He should know how to use it."

"I don't know," I said. "My mom says he comes and goes . . . whatever that means."

"Then what about your mom?" said Sam. "She gave *The Book* to your uncle Joe. Let's ask her how to work it."

"Well, she did show me this one page." I reached into my backpack and took out a dark blue book with twisting silver designs.

Sam jumped behind the corner of the gangster exhibit. "Oh no you don't. Put that thing down. It might be loaded."

"Don't worry," I said. "This is foolproof." I flipped open *The Book*. "It's called a magic square." I showed them this page:

Sam peeked around the corner. "What's so magic about that?"

"It has all nine numbers, one through nine. Add any three in a line and they always equal fifteen."

"So?"

"So all we have to do is tap the numbers of the year we want to travel to."

"What's with the zero?" said Fred.

"Magic squares don't usually have zeros, but it's here for time travel to years with a zero."

"Cool," said Fred. "Let's go."

"We could watch them build the pyramids in Egypt," I said.

Sam unfolded his Museum Worksheet. "We could go back a hundred years and find out what life was really like then."

Fred took off his Yankees hat and whacked us both on the head with it. "You dweebs. Forget studying! Let's just go goof around someplace. Someplace like . . . the future."

"I don't know," said Sam, adjusting his glasses. "In every time-travel book I ever read, people get in trouble when they go into the future. They either get caught by Time Police Robots, or they run into themselves and blow up."

"So we'll go a hundred years into the future," said Fred. "Then we can't run into ourselves. We'll be dead. Plus it will be great to see what New York looks like in a hundred years."

"1995 plus 100 equals 2095," I said and tapped out 2 . . . 0 . . . 9 . . . 5.

The magic square seemed to spin on the page. The People through Time exhibit began to fade behind a pale green mist. Mr. Chester and the rest of our class vanished. And we were gone.

When we opened our eyes, we were standing in a small room. We saw an old-fashioned phone on the desk, big round glass lamps, one of those record players with a hand crank that you see in history books, and something that looked like an overgrown vacuum cleaner looking at us.

THREE

The Vacuum Cleaner Death Droid began to blink and hum.

I closed my eyes and waited for the sound of the Death Ray blasting us into dust balls. But instead, I heard the sound of a human voice.

"Oh, there you are!"

A tall woman with dark green hair and a gown that lit up like a Christmas tree pushed aside the killer robot and grabbed Sam by the shoulders.

"Those old-fashioned sight mods are perfect."

"You like my glasses?" said Sam.

"Hey lady, what's your number?" said the nagging metal voice.

The green-haired lady let out a gasp. "Oh no. This SellBot was going to spec you?"

Fred nodded. "He had us dead in his sights."

"You didn't give it your number did you?"

"Just my phone number," I said.

"Thank goodness," said the lady.

"Hey lady—"

The lady punched a quick series of numbers on the SellBot's keypad. It turned and floated out of the room. Our rescuer turned and looked Fred over. "Where on earth did they find that antique Yankees hat? It's magnificent."

Then she spied me. "And those shoes." I looked at my beat-up, unlaced sneakers. "They look so authentic! But why are you in the 1890s room? I told the agency to have you report to the 1990s room."

Fred, Sam, and I looked at each other. We couldn't

quite figure out where we were. The lady and the robot looked like something from a hundred years in the future. Everything else looked like a hundred years in the past.

"I'm Director Green," said the lady. "I'm in charge of the Rooms of the Past exhibits." She walked over and touched the wall. A panel of tiny pictures, lines, and shapes appeared. "The exhibits open in ten minutes. Let's transport to the 1990s room and get you boys set up."

She touched the glowing part of the wall, moved four blue triangles onto the middle of a maze, then punched a blinking red arrow. The thing chirped like a cricket, and we were instantly standing in a completely different room.

"A transporter," whispered Sam. "So we must be in the future."

"Then why does it look like my bedroom?" said Fred.

We looked around and saw Fred was right. Now it looked like we were in the 1990s.

Bugs Bunny and Daffy Duck were blasting each other on the TV. A couch, and a table stacked with board games, baseball cards, papers, a pencil, and string filled the middle of the room.

"Doesn't it make you feel just like you're standing

in the middle of the twentieth century?" said Director Green.

I wondered how we could be standing in the middle of the twentieth century with robots and transporters. I wondered why Director Green looked so different but sounded so much like Mr. Chester. And that's when I figured it out.

"What's the date today?" I asked.

Director Green slid her finger across another panel. The blue numbers 9/28/95 appeared.

"September 28," she said.

"And that 95 doesn't stand for 1995 does it?"

Director Green laughed. "Only in this room. Your job is to play the way children from the 1990s might have played. Down the hall it's 2025. Then we have the 2045 room, the Swinging 2060s, and the 2075 room. For everyone else out there, it's 2095 all year long."

Fred, Sam, and I looked at each other.

We were a hundred years in the future, standing in a museum exhibit of a hundred years past.

"So we're supposed to be dummies from 1995?" said Fred.

"That shouldn't be too hard for some people I know," said Sam.

Director Green handed me a book from the shelf.

"Why don't you pretend you are scanning this. It's called a book. You've probably seen vids of people using these in the old days. Can you imagine? People used to scan the output and project stories on their own."

I looked at the book. "*Green Eggs and Ham!* That was my favorite when I was a kid."

Director Green handed Fred a remote. "And this controls the vid display. This early system was called television. No one had even thought of brain stim. Images could only be beamed to this large box. Children used to sit in front of it and file data via visual interface."

Fred took the remote and stretched out on the couch. "I'm not sure what you said, but I definitely know how to watch cartoons. This is the one where Bugs and Daffy fight over rabbit season and duck season. Watch this. Daffy's going to blow his own beak to the top of his head."

Director Green gave us a funny look. "It's wonderful that you boys know so much about the 1990s. I'll be sure to mention it to your agency." She looked around the room for something for Sam. "This would be perfect for you. It's called a pencil. You could pretend to be looking through your old-fashioned spectacles and outputting text and picture files by hand."

"You want me to doodle?" asked Sam.

"Oh, that's a perfect old slang word, too," said Director Green. "You could fool anyone into thinking they were watching three boys from the 1990s at play."

Fred, Sam, and I tried not to laugh.

"All set then," said Director Green. "The Museum of Natural History People of the Past exhibit is now officially open." She pressed a wavy red sign on the wall control panel. The wall nearest the hall disappeared, but the pictures on it stayed right where they were. "I've turned on the InvisiWall. No one can get in. Use your code numbers to get out."

She tapped a string of numbers on the control panel. A door appeared in the invisible wall and she turned to leave. But when she opened the door, our real troubles began.

Three guys in funny-looking blue jeans and fake-looking T-shirts walked into the room. "Sorry we're late. The agency sent us for the 1990s exhibit," said the kid in front.

"But that can't be," said Director Green. "You're already here."

The second kid handed a disk to Director Green. She popped it into a slot in the control panel. She looked at us, then the three kids, then us, then the three kids again.

"That is the agency contract. But if you are you, who—" she turned to us—"are they?"

FOUR

"Who are we?" repeated Sam. "Uh, we are—"

Fred stepped in front of Sam. "I'll tell you who we are. We are . . . magicians."

Director Green looked puzzled.

The three guys cheered. "Magic!"

Fred put his arm around my shoulder. "Joe, the Magnificent, will show you an amazing trick."

I gave Fred my best evil eye, then tried to think of a quick trick. I took the pencil from Sam.

"Have you ever seen anything float in midair with no support?" I said.

"Of course we have," said the lead guy. "You think we've never seen an anti-gravity disk?"

I had a sudden feeling it was going to be tough to impress kids a hundred years in the future.

"Make it disappear," said the second.

"Blow it up!" said the third.

"I can do better than that," I said. "I'll turn it to

rubber right before your very eyes." I banged the pencil on the table. "Solid, right?"

Director Green jumped. "Careful, please. There aren't many of those antiques left."

"I say the magic words three times—Banana bones, banana bones, banana bones." I held the pencil horizontal at eye level and wiggled it up and down. "Presto, it's rubber!"

My audience looked completely unimpressed.

"I can also stick the pencil through my head." I put the eraser end of the pencil in my left ear and pushed my right cheek out with my tongue. I pulled the pencil down and moved my tongue up. Pencil up, tongue down. Pencil down, tongue up.

"Can you shoot fire out of your fingers?" asked one of the kids.

"Maybe I should just run a quick check on you boys," said Director Green, looking a little nervous. I had visions of the SellBot returning.

"Wait," said Fred. "First let me show you this one magic knot trick. Stand in a circle and put your right hands together." Director Green and the three guys obeyed Fred's command. "Now close your eyes while I tie the magic knot." Fred tied their hands together and motioned us toward the door in the InvisiWall. "Count backward with me. When we reach zero, the magic knot will disappear. 60, 59, 58, 57..."

Director Green and the three guys joined in. "56, 55, 54, 53..."

Fred, Sam, and I backed slowly out the door counting. "52, 51, 50..." We found ourselves in the middle of a large room.

"I didn't know you knew magic," I said.

"I don't," said Fred. "Let's get out of here." He ran toward a stairway, then bounced back.

"Watch out for those InvisiWalls," said Sam.

I looked around for a way to escape. "I think I know where we are. This used to be where they had the African mammals. If we go down those stairs and past the North American mammals, that should put us right in the main lobby."

We could hear Director Green and the three guys still counting. "39, 38, 37. . ."

We took off running. We ran past giraffes, gorillas, and a herd of elephants. We jumped down a flight of steps, turned the corner, and ran straight into the SellBot.

"Hey buddy, what's your number?"

"Oh no. Not Hoover Head again," said Fred.

"Maybe we can overload his circuits with a giant number," said Sam.

The SellBot stuck out its number pad. Sam punched 384,621 × 489,792. The SellBot didn't pause. "188,384,288,832. Wrong number."

We heard the noise of people calling upstairs.

"So much for my magic knot," said Fred.

"Hey buddy, what's your number?"

"Okay, try these," said Sam. "Joe's number is 100 divided by 3. Fred's number is the square root of 2. And my number is pi. Calculate those, dust sucker."

The SellBot whirred and hummed. Its lights blinked. The noise upstairs got louder and closer. The SellBot made a weird pinging noise and started bumping into the wall saying, "33.333333333333 . . . *ping* . . . 1.41421356 . . . *ping* . . . 3.14159265358979323

. . . ping. . . ."

"What did you do to it?" asked Fred.

"None of those numbers end." Sam smiled. "All three go on forever."

The crazed robot hummed and pinged and crashed its head into the wall. Smoke leaked out of its side. The SellBot crashed to the ground.

That's when we heard a voice call from the top of the stairs, "There they are!"

FIVE

We jumped over the twitching SellBot and ran down a flight of stairs. We had almost made it to the lobby, when the sound of a buzzer filled the halls.

The museum doors opened. A tidal wave of people came flooding in, and we were right in its path.

We dodged the first bunch of teenagers. They had corkscrew, spike, and Mohawk hair in every color you can think of. But the most amazing thing was that no one was touching the ground.

"They're flying. People in the future have figured out how to fly," said Sam.

A solid river of people flowed past us. An old man in an aluminum suit. A woman with leopard-patterned skin. A class in shiny school uniforms. Everyone was floating about a foot above the floor.

"How do they do that?" I said.

"Look closely," said Sam. "Everyone has a small disk with a green triangle and a red square."

"Hey, you're right," I said.

"I'm always right," said Sam. "That is obviously the anti-gravity disk that kid was talking about. Now let's get out of here before another SellBot tracks us down."

Fred grabbed my belt. Sam grabbed Fred's belt. And we fought our way outside. We stopped at the statue of Teddy Roosevelt sitting on his horse looking out over Central Park. We stood and looked out with him.

"Wow," said Fred. "I see it but I don't believe it."

The sidewalk was full of floating people of every shape and color. There were people with green skin, blue skin, purple skin, orange, striped, plaid, dotted, and you-name-it skin. The street was packed three high and three deep with floating bullet-shaped things that must have been anti-gravity cars. And all around the trees of Central Park, towering buildings spread up and out like gigantic mechanical trees taller than the clouds. Layers and layers of anti-gravity cars and lines of people snaked around a hundred stories above us. New York was bigger, busier, and noisier than ever.

"Okay. I think I've seen enough of New York 2095," said Sam. "Let's hit 1995 on the magic square and head out before the killer robots show up again." Sam sat down under Teddy's horse, drew the magic square,

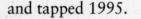

and tapped 1995.

Nothing happened.

Fred and Sam looked at me.

"Wow. Look at that building," I said.

"Hey, Mr. Book Expert," said Sam. "Our fool-proof magic square seems to be fooling us."

"Yeah," said Fred. "You said all we have to do is tap the year we want to go to."

I cleared my throat. "We have to use the magic square in *The Book,*" I said as fast as I could.

Sam looked stunned. "Tell me you're kidding." He looked at me again. "You're not kidding. This is so incredibly stupid. Even the dumbest subhumans in Demons and Dragons don't make the same mistake five times in a row. Who could be such a knucklehead?"

Fred and Sam looked at me.

"Such a chump," said Fred.

"Such a nitwit," said Sam.

"Dolt."

"Dunce."

"Okay! Okay! I get the idea," I said. "*The Book* will turn up. It's always somewhere."

"I'm not going back in that museum," said Sam. He took one step down from the statue. And then out of nowhere, the scariest-looking robot I have ever seen or even imagined appeared in front of us. It was ten feet tall, covered with weapons, and laughing an evil, metal laugh. It made the SellBot look like a toaster.

Sam jumped behind Teddy Roosevelt's horse.

"You cannot run. You cannot hide. Slayer 3000," boomed the monster robot. *"Now playing in brain stim theaters everywhere."*

The Slayer 3000 disappeared and a five-foot-tall slice of pizza appeared in its place.

"Eat Ray's Pizza Now!" said the slice. Then it disappeared too.

I looked down the sidewalk and saw robots,

pizza, beer bottles, miniature faces, and 101 different ads popping on and off above the floating
crowd. No one seemed to pay any attention.

"Wow," I said. "3-D advertising."

"I knew that," said Sam.

Sam looked over my shoulder and suddenly froze.
"Act natural. Keep talking. This is just how it hap-
pens in the time-travel movies. Just when you think
the good guys are safe, they get attacked by the
most unlikely bad guys."

"What are you talking about?" I said. "That
Slayer 3000 was just a movie ad."

"I know," said Sam. "But those three girls over
there are for real. They've been watching us and
checking a piece of paper. They're probably time
police in disguise."

"What are you talking about?" said Fred.

"Those girls," said Sam. "I'll bet they're time
travel police, working with the SellBots."

Just then, Director Green came out of the museum entrance. The SellBot was right behind her.

"You three boys—come here."

Sam and Fred and I thought about it for just one
second. Then we took off down Central Park West,
headed for Seventy-seventh Street.

SIX

"**R**un for your life," yelled Sam. "Next the killer girls will be saying they only want to help us."

We dodged another class trip in silver pajamas.

"Wait. We only want to help you," yelled one of the girls.

That was all we needed to hear. We ran twice as fast. Fred took the lead. We turned right on Seventy-seventh Street, crossed Columbus Avenue, and headed for Broadway.

"Watch where you're going!"

"Get off the flyway!"

"Buy a disk!"

"*Eat Ray's Pizza Now!*"

Everything and everybody yelled at us as we bounced off floating ads and low-flying people.

I looked back over one shoulder. The killer girls were only a block behind us, flying along effortlessly with their anti-gravity disks.

"We'll never outrun them on the ground," I panted.

"We're doomed," said Sam.

"Not yet we're not," said Fred. He pointed to a tiny shop squeezed in between ads for Jono! Breath Freshener and Dr. Lane's Deodorant Pills.

His sign said "Ray's Original Pizza and Stuff."

"We're about to die and you want a slice of pizza?" asked Sam.

Fred walked up to the shop. "I'll have a slice and three anti-gravity disks."

A little green man put a slice and three anti-gravity disks on the counter.

"We're saved," said Sam.

I looked back at the girls. I know this sounds strange, but the one in the lead wearing a baseball cap looked like Fred with a ponytail.

"That'll be $153," said the man. "One dollar for each AG patch. One hundred and fifty for the slice."

We dug in our pockets and came up with my one measly quarter. "We're doomed," said Sam.

I held the quarter in front of me between my thumbs and forefingers. "Have you ever seen a human bend metal?" I asked, hoping he might give us the disks for a trick.

The old man picked up the disks. "You ever seen a pizza guy call the cops?"

I looked back. The girls were getting closer. I got a good look at the second one, and I'm telling you—it gave me the chills. She looked like a girl version of Sam without the glasses. We had to do something to get those disks. Quick.

And that's exactly what Sam did.

"I'll just put that on my number," said Sam. The pizza guy gave Sam a nasty look.

"Why dintcha say that in the first place?" He slid Sam a number pad. Sam typed 852-159-654-753. He scooped up our disks and we ran.

"What about your slice?" called the pizza man.

We stopped at the corner of Broadway and Seventy-seventh. Stacks of car pods swooshed downtown. Lines of people snaked above us. We smelled a nasty odor. We were standing ankle deep in trash that everyone else floated over.

"What was that number you punched?" I asked.

"That's the museum number," said Sam. "It was a cinch to remember. It's four combinations on the magic square: 8+5+2, 1+5+9, 6+5+4, and 7+5+3."

"Oh yeah. That's a cinch," said Fred.

"Disks on," said Sam. We each slapped a patch on our T-shirt. "Activate green triangle now." We punched our green triangles and popped up into the flow of people-traffic above us.

"Check it out," said Fred. "To steer these things, you just look in the direction you want to go."

"Eyeball control," said Sam. "Amazing."

Traffic stopped. We floated across the street with everyone else. Over the incredible din of car pods, bus pods, talking ads, and talking people I heard someone yell, "Joe!"

I turned and saw the third girl waving. My blood froze. It was scary enough that she knew my name, but scarier still that she looked just like my sister.

"Fast forward," I yelled.

Now I know Fred had never even seen one of

these anti-gravity things before, but he sailed down the flyway like he had used an anti-gravity disk every day of his life. Sam and I followed. We surfed through crowds of people streaming out of the giant buildings. We zigzagged around jungles of singing, talking 3-D ads. But every time we looked back, the girls were still there.

"We can't shake them," said Sam. "It's like they know where we're going."

"Time to pull some stunts," said Fred.

We hit some open space down near Sixty-eighth Street, and Fred found exactly what he was looking for. A crowd of people blocked the flyway. Behind them was a talking giant 3-D toilet paper roll. If you were a maniac, you might think it was a ramp to jump over the crowd.

"Time to catch some air," yelled Fred the maniac.

Killer girls behind us. Solid crowd in front of us. We had no choice but to follow Fred in the only direction left. Up.

"*Squishy Soft is oh, so smooth,*" said the toilet paper roll.

We flew down the toilet paper, up the roll, and into midair over the crowd. And we probably would have landed just as smoothly, but we ran into a little problem. A squishy-soft problem. Right

where Fred was planning to land, there was another talking roll of Squishy Soft.

We hit the second roll, one, two, three, bounced high in the air, then fell to the ground hopelessly tangled in "Oh, so smooth" Squishy Soft.

SEVEN

I heard the crowd, felt someone unwrap us, heard Sam moan, "I'm too young to die."

Fred, Sam, and I spilled out of the Squishy Soft wrapping. We were right in the middle of a small stage. And the entire crowd was staring at us, pointing, laughing, and clapping.

"Presto chango alakazam," boomed a voice behind us. And the minute I heard that voice, I knew who it was.

"Uncle Joe!"

"We're saved," said Sam.

Uncle Joe looked at me, the crowd, then back at me. "Joe? You're not a rabbit."

"No," I said. "At least I don't think I am."

Uncle Joe looked over at Sam and Fred. "And they're not doves."

Sam and Fred shook their heads no.

Uncle Joe looked in his top hat. "I can never get
that trick to work quite right."

Someone yelled, "On with the show."

"You've got to hide us, quick," I said. "The time
police are chasing us."

Uncle Joe twirled his moustache. Then he
wrapped the three of us in Squishy Soft.

"Ladies and gentleman, believers and friends. For
my final feat of prestidigitation, I will need your un-
divided attention. With your help, I will send these
three wrapped lads into the warp of Time and
Space, never to be seen again."

Sam wiggled next to me. "Is he serious?"

4 1

"No," I said. "He can't do that. He'll probably drop us through a trapdoor in the stage."

"I'll need three volunteers," said Uncle Joe. "Ah yes. You three young ladies in the back."

I had a slight sinking feeling. I peeked through a hole in our Squishy Soft wrapping.

"Oh no," I said. "Guess who he picked?"

"The killer girls," said Fred.

"What do we do?" squeaked Sam.

"Stay calm," I said. "Maybe Uncle Joe's trick will work and they won't spot us."

"And maybe an elephant with wings will fly out of my nose," said Sam.

"The human mind is a powerful instrument," boomed Uncle Joe. "Imagine how powerful a group of minds could be. With the help of these three young ladies, we will join minds and disintegrate this . . . toilet paper!"

"I don't feel so good," whispered Sam.

"Our first volunteer will chant 'Ee-Nee.' The second will chant 'Me-Nee.' The third will chant 'My-Nee.' Then everyone join in to chant 'Mo.' As soon as we have merged our thoughts, I will flush the toilet paper into Time and Space."

Someone in the crowd yelled, "Why don't you use a toilet transporter?"

"I work by brain power alone," said Uncle Joe. Then he pointed to the first girl.

She said, "Ee-Nee."

He pointed to the second girl.

She said, "Me-Nee."

The third girl.

She said, "My-Nee."

The crowd shouted, "*Mo!*"

"EeNee."

"MeNee."

"MyNee."

"*Mo!*"

"Ee-Nee-Me-Nee-My-Nee-*Mo!*"

"EeNeeMeNeeMyNee*Mo!*"

Uncle Joe raised both arms. There was a flash of light, a crash, and a huge white puff of smoke.

"Ladies and gentlemen, where there once were three boys, I give you—"

A blast of wind from a passing bus pod blew the smoke away and revealed . . . Fred, Sam, and me. The only thing that had disappeared was our Squishy Soft disguise.

One of the girls called, "There they are."

A metal voice behind us said, "Hey buddy, what's your number?"

Uncle Joe said, "Ooops."

43

EIGHT

"Hey buddy, what's your number?" said the Sell-Bot.

"This is getting monotonous," said Sam.

But before we could even worry about getting out of this latest trap, the three girls took charge. The one with the baseball cap picked up the Squishy Soft roll and stuffed it over the SellBot.

"Hey buddy, what's your number?" said the muffled voice of the blinded SellBot.

"*Squishy Soft is oh, so smooth,*" said the roll.

"Come on," said the girl who looked like my sister. "Follow us."

Sam looked at Fred. Fred looked at me. I looked at Uncle Joe.

"Do we have any choice?" I asked.

We took off and followed the girls around buildings, over crowds of crazily colored people, past streamlined pods and more talking, blinking, singing 3-D ads, until I had no idea where we were. We finally stopped in front of a building too tall to believe.

"Here's my house," said the lead girl.

Fred, Sam, and I looked up and up and up at the building that disappeared in the clouds.

The girl led us through a triangle door that opened at her voice. She put her hand over a blinking red handprint on the wall. And in five seconds we were all transported to a room that must have been five miles above New York City.

The girls flopped down on cushions. "This is my room," said the girl who looked like my sister.

We stood nervously in one corner.

"So you're not killer time cops?" I said.

The three girls looked at me like I was crazy.

"Of course not," said one.

"Whatever gave you that idea?" said another.

Then we all started asking questions.

"Who are you guys?"

"Why did you save us?"

"How did you know we'd be at the museum?"

"Do you have anything to eat?"

The girls laughed. The one who led us there pushed a green dot on a small table. A bowl of something looking like dried green dog food appeared with a pile of liquid filled plastic balls. "Here's some Vitagorp and Unicola," said the girl who looked like my sister. "Now let me try to explain things from the beginning."

We copied the girls and sucked on the plastic ball things the same way they did. Fred ate a handful of the green dog food.

"I'm Joanie. This is Samantha. That's Frieda."

"But everybody calls me Freddi," said the girl with the baseball hat.

"And we have these names," Joanie continued, "because we

were named after our great-grandfathers—Joe, Sam, and Fred."

"Or in other words—you," said Samantha.

Everything suddenly made sense. That's why they looked so much like us.

"Of course," said Uncle Joe, dusting off his top hat. "Your great-grandkids have to make sure you get back to 1995. Otherwise you won't have kids. Then your kids won't have kids. Then your kids' kids won't have—"

"Us," said Samantha. "Your great-grandkids. And we knew you would be at the museum because you wrote us a note." Samantha handed me a yellowed sheet of paper that had been sealed in plastic. It was our Museum Worksheet from 1995. On the back was a note in my handwriting that said:

Girls,

Meet us under Teddy Roosevelt's statue at the Museum of Natural History, September 28, 2095.

Sincerely,
Joe, Sam, Fred

"How did you get our worksheet from 1995?" asked Sam.

"I got it from my mom," said Joanie. "And she got it from her mom."

"But we didn't write that," I said.

"You will," said Samantha, "if we can get you back to 1995."

"Saved by our own great-grandkids with a note we haven't written yet?" said Sam. "I told you something like this was going to happen. Now we're probably going to blow up."

"Wow," said Fred, eating more Vitagorp. "Our own great-grandkids. So what team is that on your hat? I've never seen that logo."

"That's the Yankees," said Freddi. "They changed it when Grandma was pitching."

"Your grandma? Fred's daughter?" I said. "A pitcher for the Yankees?"

"Not just a pitcher. She was a great pitcher," said Freddi. "2.79 lifetime ERA, 275 wins, 3 no-hitters, and the Cy Young award in '37."

"Forget your granny's stats," said Sam. "We could be genius inventors back in 1995 if we could reconstruct these levitation devices."

"What did he just say?" asked Freddi.

"He wants to know how the anti-gravity disks

work," said Samantha. "A truly amazing discovery. More surprising than Charles Goodyear's accidental discovery of vulcanized rubber. More revolutionary than Alexander Graham Bell's first telephone. But all I can tell you is that the anti-gravity power comes from the chemical BHT. And it was discovered in a breakfast accident."

"What's a breakfast accident?" said Sam. "A head-on collision with a bowl of cornflakes? And who found out BHT could make things fly?"

"You did," said Samantha. "That's why we can't tell you more. You know the Time Warp Info-Speed Limit posted in *The Book*. Anyone traveling through time with too much information from another time blows up."

Sam's eyes nearly bugged out of his head. "I knew it. Don't tell me another word."

"Hey, wait a minute," I said. "Where did you say that info-speed limit was?"

Samantha looked at me like I was an insect.

"In *The Book,* of course."

"How do you know about *The Book*?"

"I got it for my birthday last year," said Joanie.

"And since then we've been all over time," said Freddi. "We've met cavewomen, Ann the Pirate, Calamity Jane . . ."

"And don't forget Cleopatra and the underground cities of Venus," said Samantha.

"But if you have *The Book,* that means we're saved," said Sam.

Samantha gave Sam her look. "If you remember the Time Warpers' Tips, you know nothing can be in two places at once. Of course our *Book* disappeared as soon as your *Book* appeared."

"So now we have to help you get *The Book* back to the past," said Freddi, "so we can have it in the future."

"Of course," said Sam.

"We knew that," said Fred.

"Uh, right . . ." I said, trying to talk my way out of this mess. "We knew that would happen, but we uh . . ." I looked around at Sam, Fred, Samantha, Freddi, and Joanie. Then I spotted Uncle Joe. "We thought we could really learn some tricks about finding *The Book* from Uncle Joe!"

Uncle Joe looked up from something he was fiddling with in his lap. "*The Book*? Oh, I never could get it to work the way your mother did. That's why I gave it to you for your birthday."

"Oh, great," said Sam. "We're doomed."

"But that's also why I put this together." Uncle Joe held up the thing he had been fiddling with in his lap. It was an old-fashioned pocket watch. "My Time Warp Watch."

"We're saved!" yelled Sam.

NINE

"I was on my way to 1920 to see if the great Houdini could advise me on a particularly puzzling prestidigitation. A minor miscalculation landed me here in 2095 instead." Uncle Joe wound the knob on the top of his watch. "But now that I've tightened the past spring and loosened the future spring, I am prepared to disembark once again. If you boys would care to accompany me, I would be delighted to deposit you at your destination en route to my aforementioned rendezvous with the master of illusion."

"What did he say?" asked Fred.

"He said he'd drop us off in 1995 on his way to meet Houdini," I said.

"We never did get a chance to taste any 2095 pizza," said Fred. "But I guess we'd better go."

I turned to Joanie, Freddi, and Samantha. "Well . . . it was nice to meet you, and uh . . . thanks for saving us."

Uncle Joe flipped open the cover on the watch. "Tempus fugit. Alakazam." He spun the hands backward, and the four of us started to spin.

"Wait," said Samantha. "*The Book* is probably—"

Sam plugged his ears and started talking as loud as he could. "I'm not listening. La la la. I can't hear you. La la la. No more information."

Fred, Sam, and I swirled up in time and space behind Uncle Joe. Then we were gone.

TEN

I remember thinking Uncle Joe's time warping was a little rougher than we were used to. We spun and bumped and finally came to rest.

That's when we got our first surprise.

We weren't standing in the middle of New York. We were sitting in the tops of three coconut trees. A parrot flew by. The sun beat down. The ocean waves crashed.

"I think I'm going to throw up," said Sam.

"This place looks kind of familiar," I said.

"Oh no," said Sam.

"Are you going to toss your cookies?" asked Fred.

"Vomit your victuals?" asked Uncle Joe.

Sam pointed to the ocean behind us.

We turned around and saw a huge wooden ship sail out from behind the rocks. This ship had a flag with a familiar-looking white skull.

Fred said the one word that said it all.

"Blackbeard."

Uncle Joe balanced in the tree with the watch in one hand and his top hat in the other. "Maybe I should loosen the past spring." He twisted the dial. "Tempus fugit. Alakazam."

The world swirled. I heard the awful sound I recognized as Blackbeard singing.

Lights, sound, and images twirled past. I felt like I was on one of those nasty carnival rides that twists and spins at the same time. We stopped with a thud. I couldn't see anything in the cloud of dust.

"Fred? Sam? Uncle Joe? Are you there?"

"I'm going to upchuck," said Sam's voice.

"Buick?" said Fred's voice.

"Regurgitate?" said Uncle Joe's voice.

We heard a distant moo. We smelled the unmistakable odor that follows a herd of cattle. Then we knew exactly where we were.

"Or maybe I should have tightened the future spring," said the voice of Uncle Joe.

A bugle sounded. Someone yelled, "Cavalry, charge!" Indians whooped. Cattle mooed. The earth started to rumble in an unnatural way.

"Stampede!" yelled Fred.

"Tempus fugit. Alakazam," said Uncle Joe. And we twirled up and away once more. We spun around in time and space for what seemed like hours. Strange scenes floated by like bits of dreams. When we finally stopped, our bodies landed five minutes ahead of our brains and stomachs.

"Now I am definitely going to drive the porcelain bus," said Sam.

"Toss a sidewalk pizza?" said Fred.

"Perform peristaltic pyrotechnics?" said Uncle Joe.

My head stopped spinning. I looked around to see what I already knew. We were definitely not in New

York. And we were nowhere near 1995. A forest of strange trees and giant ferns rose behind us. A volcano smoked in front of us.

"I've got it," said Uncle Joe. "I should loosen both the past spring and the future spring."

The volcano belched. Volcanic ash rained down on our heads.

"Kill me now," moaned Sam. "Throw me in the volcano. Squash me into woolly mammoth toe jam. But don't time-warp torture me again."

Uncle Joe twisted his watch, called "Tempus fugit. Alakazam," and we were off again.

This time we saw stars. We heard comets sizzle past. We twirled down drains, squeezed through pinholes, and tumbled down the stairs of history. Cavemen, pyramids, wars and kings, cities and jungles, suns and moons zipped by at blender speed. We spun faster and faster. Everything started to blur. I saw a hand and grabbed it.

The next thing I remember is looking up to see a face saying, "Joe. Joe. Are you okay?" Someone was holding my hand, helping me sit up.

My brain slowly cleared, and I saw that it was Joanie. We were back exactly where we had started—Joanie's room, New York, 2095. Uncle Joe was nowhere to be seen. Freddi was helping Fred sit up. Samantha was holding Sam's glasses while he leaned over an empty flowerpot.

"Now would you like me to tell you where *The Book* probably is?" said Samantha.

Sam looked up, squinted, and lost his lunch.

ELEVEN

The six of us stood under Theodore Roosevelt's statue in front of the museum. We looked like three goofy sets of boy-girl twins. Sam and Samantha. Fred and Freddi. Joe and Joanie. Crowds of people streamed past.

"Man do I feel stupid in this doofy outfit," said Fred.

"We're just lucky my little brother is not so little. Now you blend in," said Freddi. "Except for that antique Yankees hat. Give me that and I'll hide it." Freddi reached for Fred's hat.

Fred jumped back. "Nobody touches my hat."

"Okay. Knock it off," said Joanie. "Let's go over the plan one more time."

I picked at my suit. The material was so light it didn't feel like anything. That, and the fact that it had somehow fixed itself on me without buttons or zippers or anything, made me a little nervous about walking around in public.

Joanie traced the plan on the palm of her hand. "We go in first and set up near the 1990s room. You wait fifteen minutes, then meet us up there. Samantha knocks out the InvisiWall. You three run in, get *The Book* from one of the bookshelves, then fly out of there."

"How do you know *The Book* will be there?" said Sam.

"Simple logic," said Samantha. "You are looking for *The Book*. You wrote a note telling us to meet you at the museum. The 1990s room is the only room that has books. Therefore, *The Book* is in the 1990s room."

"Girls," said Sam.

"You're lucky we came and rescued you," said Freddi. "Otherwise you'd still be time tumbling."

"We don't really need help," said Fred. "We knew where we were."

"Boys," said Freddi.

"Let's just get *The Book* so you can get back to the past, and we can get our *Book* back in the future," said Joanie.

Joanie, Samantha, and Freddi disappeared into the museum. We looked out over Central Park. The orange ball of the sun was going down behind the dense forest of buildings crowding the sky.

"*Try Dr. Lane's,*" said a pill drifting by.

"*Eat Ray's original pizza now!*" said a slice hanging over Roosevelt's head. "*Vitagorp,*" said a green bag. "*Unicola,*" said a tennis ball.

"Can you believe people used to live like that?" said a lady floating out of the museum.

"No SensaTheater? No brain stim?" said the purple man next to her. "How did they stand it back in the twentieth century?"

"You know it's kind of amazing to see the twenty-first century," I said. "But I sure will be glad to get back to the twentieth century."

"Me too," said Fred. "Let's do it."

We hopped down from the statue base and drifted in with the crowd. Groups of kids gathered in the lobby under the huge skeleton. We joined a bunch about our age, and pretended to be listening to the teacher.

". . . which some people didn't even believe existed. Does anyone know it's name? It says *Loch nessasaurus* on the plaque. Right."

"The Loch Ness Monster," whispered Sam. "Let's ask if they've found the Abominable Snowman."

"Now we'll go in and look at the exhibits that

show how people lived from 1960 up to the 2060s. Take a look and think about what things have changed in a hundred years. Stay together. You can either take notes for your work screen, or brain in the complete answers as we go. Questions? No, you cannot check out the rubber ants in the gift shop. Okay, let's go."

"Stick with this class," I whispered. "This is perfect." Twenty minutes later, I realized that maybe this wasn't so perfect. Mr. Zechter (the teacher) was still telling us everything he knew (and didn't know) about the sixties.

"... they wore pants called bell bottoms, and

listened to music by a group called The Bugs. They worshipped bright images and made symbols they believed had power over wars and peace."

"I can't take it anymore," said Sam.

I had a flash of inspiration. I raised my hand.

"Yes?" said Mr. Zechter.

I grabbed Sam's head and bent him over. "Sam doesn't feel good. I think he's going to barf."

"Vomit?" said Mr. Zechter.

"Puke?" said a kid in front of me.

"Odor chunk output?" said a kid next to me.

Mr. Zechter looked panicked.

"I better take him to the bathroom," I said.

"Please," said Mr. Zechter, looking relieved.

Fred and I grabbed Sam between us and dragged him down the hall.

By the time we got to the 1990s room, we were fifteen minutes late. The three girls looked ready to kill us.

Joanie gave us the sign. We pushed up against the InvisiWall. Then everything happened so fast that we didn't have time to think. Samantha typed something into the wall controls, and suddenly we were leaning against nothing.

"Go, go, go!" said Fred.

We ran into the room and each one of us took a

shelf as planned. I could hear Joanie and Freddi making a scene behind us so everyone looked at them instead of us.

"*Treasure Island, Conan, Robinson Crusoe, Men from Mars*—it's not here," said Fred.

"*Green Eggs and Ham, World's Greatest Jokes and Riddles, Robin Hood, Legends of King Arthur*—it's not here," said Sam.

My heart was pounding and I felt like I could barely breathe as I flipped through the books.

"*Grimms' Fairy Tales, Tarzan, The Stinky Cheese Man, White Fang*—it's not here either."

"You boys. Just what do you three think you are doing in there? Get out this instant." It was Mr. Zechter. He'd finally made it to the 1990s.

"It's got to be here somewhere," said Fred. We ran around the room like maniacs, diving under the couch, rolling back rugs, flipping papers, cards, checkers, and baseballs into the air.

"Boys," said Mr. Zechter. "*Boys!*"

"Forget it," I said. "*The Book*'s not here. Let's make a break for it."

We activated our AG disks and took off. Sam and I were zooming past Mr. Zechter when I heard that voice I never want to hear again.

"Hey buddy, what's your number?"

Fred was still in the room, looking through the desk. "Come on, *Book*. Where are you?"

Fred didn't see the robot raise its laser. Everything happened too fast for Sam and me to do anything. But somehow Freddi dove into the room, grabbed the baseball, and whipped a strike that knocked the SellBot's laser flying.

The SellBot pulled a trigger in the empty air.

Sam and I flew down the hall one way. Samantha and Joanie made a break the other way.

And we probably would have made it all the way outside. But when we turned the corner at the top of the stairs, we looked back and saw a sight that sank all of our plans for escape.

Standing in the 1990s room with their hands up against the InvisiWall were Fred and his great-granddaughter-who-might-never-be, Freddi.

TWELVE

"Being interested in books is one thing," said Director Green. "But destroying museum exhibits is quite another."

Fred, Sam, and I sat on the couch in the 1990s room. Freddi, Samantha, and Joanie sat by the desk. We were caught. We were being lectured.

"This collection of books was donated by a famous man years ago. He left very specific instructions that the collection be kept together and always visible to the public." Director Green put her hands on her hips and looked at each of us in turn. "If anything had happened to any one of those books, it would have been a terrible thing. Do you understand that?"

We all looked at our shoes and answered together, "Yes, ma'am."

A museum guard called from the hall, "Director Green, could I see you for a minute?"

"I want you to think about what you've done," said Director Green, and she walked out.

"It must be here," said Samantha.

"Forget it," said Sam. "*The Book* will turn up. It always does. But what magic did you use to short out the InvisiWall with just a number?"

"Well, you see," said Samantha, "the magnetic circuitry transference modulator—"

"Wait a minute. Never mind," said Sam. "Just in case we do find *The Book* and get home, I'd better stay below the info-speed limit."

Fred looked at Freddi and kicked her foot. "That was a great throw to save me from that killer robot. You want to trade hats?"

Freddi somehow knew that this was the greatest compliment Fred could ever give anyone. She handed Fred her 2095 Yankees cap and put his 1995 Yankees cap on. "Aw, it wasn't that dangerous. I just didn't want you to get trapped by that thing shooting out sale items with its hololaser."

"Sale items? You mean those SellBots don't shoot death lasers?" I asked. "What about all that 'What's your number' stuff?"

"Once they get your credit number, they shoot out 3-D sale ads until you buy something," said

Joanie. "It's awful."

"A SellBot just sells things?" said Sam. "Why didn't you tell us?"

"You never asked," said Samantha.

Luckily Director Green walked back in just then. She had a funny look on her face. "Extraordinary. . . ." Then she spoke to Joanie. "I've just spoken with the museum head. Your uncle Joe has explained everything."

We all perked up.

"Uncle Joe? Has explained everything?" I said. "Er . . . what I mean is—oh good."

I was trying to imagine how Uncle Joe made it

back to 2095 to explain why we were tearing apart the 1990s room in the Museum of Natural History, when Director Green turned to Joanie. "Why didn't you tell me that it was your great-grandfather who donated these books?"

"I . . ." Joanie looked just as surprised as I felt. "I . . . didn't think you would believe me."

"Oh," said Director Green. "But these books . . ." And the minute she said the word, it was like someone had waved a magic wand over her. "These books are amazing! There's Tarzan gliding silently through the jungle canopy." Director Green swung on an imaginary vine. "And Sir Galahad when he smote down horse and man in one stroke." She swung a two-handed blow at the desk and chair. "Or Long John Silver tricking young Jim Hawkins." She gave a pretty good pirate's *Yaaarrr!*

"But the strangest thing happened today. I found a book in the collection that I had never seen before. Maybe you can tell me where your great-grandfather got it."

Director Green reached into a pocket in her gown and pulled out a thin blue book with twisting silver designs. "It has a very strange title—"

Fred, Sam, and I shouted in unison, *"The Book!"*

"Why, yes. How did you know?"

Director Green opened *The Book*. "It has such strange pages. Like this one with numbers in a square." She handed me *The Book*, and turned to talk to Samantha.

A thin green mist swirled around our couch.

We waved a silent good-bye to Joanie, Samantha, and Freddi as the green mist rose higher.

I whispered to Joanie, "See you in some other time."

And we left Director Green to wonder, and our great-granddaughters to explain, how we had vanished into the thin green air behind her.

T H I R T E E N

Compared to our last time tumble, this ride was first class. We sailed smoothly through the years and landed with barely a bump. Everything was back to normal for the Time Warp Trio.

Or so we thought, until the green mist dissolved, and we found ourselves staring down the barrel of a machine gun pointed directly at us.

"Oh, no," said Sam. "Not again."

"Fred, Sam, Joe!"

"They even know our names," said Fred.

"Just what do you boys think you are doing? Get out of there this instant," the voice said.

We turned around and saw our teacher.

"Mr. Chester!" said Fred.

"We're in the 1920s room," said Sam.

"I see that," said Mr. Chester. "And if you don't get out of the 1920s room and get to work now, you will be on permanent display in the afterschool room."

We climbed out of the Roaring Twenties gangster exhibit.

"Yes," said Fred. "We're back."

"Back in 1995," I said.

"No thanks to you," said Sam. Then he pointed to *The Book*. "And don't even think about using that thing again until you've read every rule in there. We could have been killed if I'd found out what BHT was."

"Well at least I donated my favorite books to the museum when I was old," I said.

"And we'd better write that note to the girls right now," said Sam. "So they can find us at the statue like they did."

"Right," said Fred. "Because if we don't write it now they won't get it then to save us before now . . . or after then?"

We thought about how impossible that was for a second. Then we cracked up laughing.

Mr. Chester failed to see the humor in the situation and made us each write an extra Museum Worksheet.

MUSEUM WORKSHEET

1) What did you learn about how to live in the past from how people live in the future?

2) List 5 inventions we use today that people didn't use 100 years ago.

3) List 5 inventions people might use 100 years from now that we don't use today.

4) List 5 synonyms for throw up.

5) How big was the largest pizza ever made?

6) Where would you find BHT at the breakfast table?

7) What do you want from the Museum gift shop?

Jon Scieszka collaborated with Lane Smith on *The Stinky Cheese Man and Other Fairly Stupid Tales*, a Caldecott Honor Book; the ALA Notable Book *The True Story of the Three Little Pigs!*; and their most recent book, *Math Curse*, in addition to the four previous *Time Warp Trio* books. Mr. Scieszka is also the author of *The Frog Prince, Continued*, a *New York Times* Notable Book, and *The Book That Jack Wrote*. He lives in Brooklyn, New York. He hopes that someone in the year 2095 will remember that his last name is pronounced *shé-ska*.

Lane Smith also wrote and illustrated *The Happy Hocky Family*, *Glasses (Who Needs 'Em?)*, and *The Big Pets*. He has won the Golden Apple of Bratislava, the Silver Buckeye, the Silver Medal of the Society of Illustrators, and many other futuristic metallic awards. He lives in New York City.